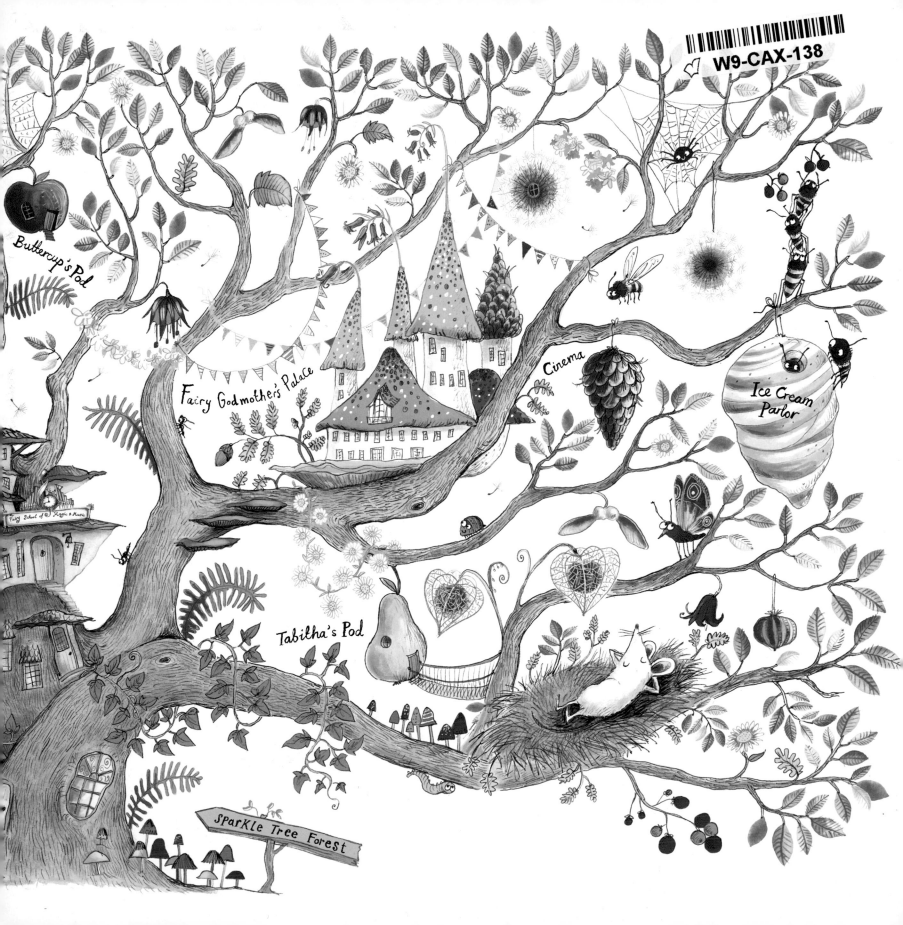

To all the children in the world who
believe in fairies and magic. K.H.

To Hilary, who shakes the fairy dust. S.W.

Sandy Creek
NEW YORK

An Imprint of Sterling Publishing
1166 Avenue of the Americas
New York, NY 10036

Text © 2014 by Katharine Holabird, Illustrations © 2014 by Sarah Warburton

This 2014 edition published by Sandy Creek. All rights reserved.

ISBN 978-1-4351-5628-9

Manufactured in China

Lot #:
2 4 6 8 10 9 7 5 3
04/15

Twinkle

Katharine Holabird · Sarah Warburton

Sandy Creek
NEW YORK

Twinkle's wings were glowing with excitement!

"Tra-la-la-la-la!" she sang. "I'm a little fairy with sparkling wings. When I get my magic wand, I'll do amazing things!"

It was Twinkle's first day at
The Fairy School of Magic and Music
and she couldn't wait to learn fancy
spells like all the big fairies.

Twinkle skipped in line with all the little fairies waiting for wands.

Her wish came true when she got a sparkling peachy pink one!

Shiny fairy notebooks and glittery pens appeared on all the desks.

"We'll start with a simple spell," said Miss Flutterbee.

"Abracadabra, skiddle-dee-dee, this stool will now become a..."

...*tree!*"

Before she could blink, Twinkle found herself perched way
up in a pear tree with Pippa and Lulu waving below.

"Now it's your turn,"
said Miss Flutterbee to the class.

Pippa and Lulu swooooshed
their wands and bingo!

They were both happily
dangling from a plum tree.

Twinkle tried swooshing her wand
but she got it all wrong, and instead of
sitting in a plum tree she landed
upside
down
in a prickly holly bush!

"Ouch!" cried Twinkle,
and Miss Flutterbee had to rescue her.

"Now remember to practice at home," said
Miss Flutterbee. "But **no** spells at night
– you don't want to start a ruckus."

That afternoon, Twinkle
and her friends did their
homework together.

"This is fun!"
said Pippa,
turning a teapot

into a tiara.

"I love doing spells,"
said Lulu, changing

bananas
into balloons.

But Twinkle's swooshes were rather clumsy, and so her spells just got sillier and **sillier.**

"Don't worry, Twinks," said Pippa and Lulu, "we can practice again tomorrow."

That night,
Twinkle was in such
a tizzy she couldn't
sleep a wink, and she
forgot all about
Miss Flutterbee's
warning.

"Fairies **never** give up!" Twinkle said to herself.
She leapt out of bed and waved her wand like Pippa and Lulu,
but she couldn't quite remember the magic words...

"Abraca-
dabbler,
Fiddle Tee-tee!"

Her wings fluttered wildly
as the bed began swinging,

the rocking chair
started rocking,

the alarm clock kept ringing,
and the lights were flashing.

Twinkle's cosy little fairy pod was shaking
and swaying, banging and clanging.

"HELP!" shouted Twinkle as the rumpus continued.

One by one all the creatures in Sparkle Tree Forest woke up, and they were not very happy… Bumble bees and ladybirds buzzed, grumpy gremlins and bullfrogs croaked, and groggy birds and bats fell out of the trees.

"Whoooooo's making that racket?" screeched the owl.

"Stop the ruckus!" shouted the squirrel.

"**Fiddlesticks and Fairy cakes!**"
said Twinkle, waving her wand faster and faster, but the crashing and banging only got louder.

The next morning, every creature in the forest was
howling and complaining outside Twinkle's door.

"Sorry about my silly spells," said Twinkle,
and she dashed off to see Miss Flutterbee.

"Gracious gremlins!" said Miss Flutterbee in surprise when she saw the parade of insects and animals following Twinkle.

"I'm having a little trouble with my homework," said Twinkle. "I keep forgetting the magic words!"

"Since you love to sing, try **singing** your spells instead.
Maybe that will help you remember," suggested Miss Flutterbee kindly.

"Brilliant!" said Twinkle,
and her wings glowed
bright pink again.

After school that day, Twinkle flew home singing the magic words.

"Abracadabra, skidddle-dee-dee, fix the mess that's up in my tree."

And when she arrived, Twinkle was overjoyed to
see everything was back in its place again.

As the sun set over Sparkle Tree Forest, Twinkle sprinkled fairy dust over the treetops and sang a lullaby to all the forest creatures, just to make sure they all had a really good sleep.

"Good night, sleep tight, with sweet dreams in your head."

Tomorrow we'll have lots of fun, but now it's time for bed!"

Lulu's Pod

Izzybell's Pod

Twinkle's Pod

Petal's Pod

Pippa's Pod

Gallery

Wand shop

Miss Flutterbee's Pod

Café

Dress Shops

Library